Always Another Twist

Sarah Leavesley

First Published in the UK in 2018 by Mantle Arts

Copyright © Sarah Leavesley 2018

The right of Sarah Leavesley to be identified as author of this work has been asserted by her.

This book is sold subject to the condition that it shall not, by the way of trade or otherwise, be lent, resold, hired out, or otherwise circulated without the publisher's prior consent in any form of binding or cover other than that in which it is published and without a similar condition, including this condition, being imposed on the subsequent purchaser.

ISBN 978-1-9998416-2-1

Mantle Lane Press
Springboard Centre
Mantle Lane
Coalville
LE67 3DW
www.mantlelanepress.co.uk
www.mantlearts.org.uk

Printed and bound in the UK by
Imprint Digital, Upton Pyne, Exeter, EX5 5HY

Cover illustration by Cindel Oranday
www.cindel.co.uk

To love, life and laughter,
and all those I've shared these with.

Ten Green Bottles Standing on a Wall

Betrayal always has a name, Julie sees that now. This name as familiar as a best friend's or partner's. But, once betrayal has a name: Lucy, it also has a face that can be made to cry, a heart that will bleed.

After discovering what her boss, Lucy, has been up to, Julie's a cauldron of anger and frustration. She has to steady her arm against the door frame as she twists the key to get into her flat.

"Screw you," Julie thinks, pouring a glass of Merlot and gulping back a large mouthful.

Glass in one hand, she pins up a pixelated print-out of her boss's snarky face. Then she picks up one of her ex-flatmate's darts and aims. The stark feathers that sprout from Lucy's bright red lips are as brittle as her lies and false promises. The next throw hits Julie's boss between the eyes.

Lost in thought, Julie's third dart catches the drawing pin instead of the photo, knocking Lucy's smile to the floor.

It was stupid to have trusted the bitch, Julie realises. She knew Lucy was a bullshitter, heard the rumours that Lucy was sleeping with her own manager 'Nick the nasty' but assumed her boss was more the victim than a driven plotter. With hindsight, Julie tots up the tell-tale signs that she missed.

When Julie first arrived at Ploughfields, she thought she'd fly high, as if she had paper-clip wings tacked to her 2:1, "a bright future", "dazzling intern" back. It had taken her a couple of jobs to work out where she wanted to go but she was sure she had more than enough steel in her to make it to the top in this world, especially with Lucy as her line manager. Lucy wasn't much older than her, she'd get where Julie was coming from.

Lucy did get where she was coming from, promised they'd rise together and watch each other's backs, despite the mountains of electronic paperwork, shifting goals and 'earthquake' files. Swapping passwords, at Lucy's suggestion, meant they could cover for each other while taking the odd sneaky coffee break. Julie happily offered her friend small eureka insights when she came to Julie with problems that needed solving. But helping out a mate was one thing, stealing Julie's own projects quite another.

Lucy's last-minute campaign brainwave 'Green is the New Black' was word-for-word, pixel-for-pixel, the same as Julie's own project plan and designs. As soon as Julie opened the file, everything changed. The familiar aspects of Lucy's past light-bulb moments, that Julie had dismissed at the time as 'great minds think alike' sparks of creative synchronicity, suddenly felt sharply and obviously calculated.

Word-for-word, pixel-for-pixel, the same as Julie's own, only the file heading changed to Lucy's name. To Lucy's name. As Lucy's own work. Simply thinking about it, Julie's fingers curl to a fist. She hadn't even mentioned her idea in passing. The only way Lucy could have taken it was if she'd actively been looking for designs to steal.

Nick loved the idea. The board loved the idea, and they loved Lucy. There was champagne, even mention of promotion. Lucy was the epitome of smiles and "it's nothing…" as the whole department flocked to congratulate her. Sipping the cold bubbles, Julie waited for some small acknowledgement, a few words of thanks, or "Without Julie this might never…" Nothing.

Okay, Julie reasons for the nth time, it's not like she and Lucy are best mates or have known each other since childhood. But they'd shared goals, Lucy nodding encouragingly. They'd moaned about work dos, laughed over ex-boyfriends' worst habits, loaned each other tights. She'd even lent Lucy her Karma Queen lipstick for that important meeting and…

Still nothing.

Pulling her thoughts away from reliving the betrayal, Julie forces herself to focus instead on 'what now?' She picks up the darts, retrieves Lucy's picture from the dust under the sofa, pins it back up on the wall and aims again. Julie throws, pointed-steel-arc-and-thud after pointed-steel-arc-and-thud, until her boss's face is blistered by tiny holes, a bitter braille of pain, and revenge.

"You should let it go, Julie," Her dad's characteristically calm advice is offered alongside a steaming cup of tea.

"Thank you, Dad, but no!"

"But are you sure? Isn't this normal for a boss?"

"To pass my ideas on. Not to pretend they're her own! It's creative. We work on an open door basis, and trust."

"But what if the plan backfires?"

"I've been through it with friends. It's fair and it's simple, hinged solely on Lucy's own underhand plotting. If this is just a one-off, a forgetting, a mistake, then nothing will happen. But if it is deliberate, a tactic..."

"I don't get how she thought you wouldn't realise."

"Nor me. Maybe she doesn't care. Or she thinks I'll have to let it go. Like you said, she is my boss. If I complain to HR, it's my word against hers. That's why this plan is better."

"If your mum were here..."

"I know, Dad. I miss her too."

Her dad stares into his mug, swilling the milky brew as if tea leaves might appear, rising to the surface along with the right words.

"Don't let this change you!" he adds as she gulps back her last mouthful and stands up to leave.

"It won't, Dad, I promise." Julie kisses his cheek reassuringly, though her thoughts are more scalding and stewed than the tea.

It isn't Lucy changing her, more that Julie's adapting. Nothing and no one stays the same forever and she clearly needs to harden up in order to survive, Julie tells herself. She uploads her 'Eureka!' project proposal to her 'PRIVATE' folder and slides a printed draft into her top drawer.

Julie hopes her opening and closing paragraphs will be more than enough to hook Lucy. Having spent the past few weeks perfecting the pitch at home, Julie would have been ready to send it as her own project. But this is more important. Two-thirds of the way through Julie has slipped in a new paragraph ranting about unfair bosses, Nick cheating on his wife and how he should really be with Lucy. Lucy would never read that far into the file before sending it. Nick the nasty probably wouldn't either. But the board would.

"I've just finished drafting a project, gonna go for lunch." Julie pauses at Lucy's desk on her way out. "I'm leaving the laptop. Can you keep an eye on it?"

"Sure, hon," Lucy smiles sweetly. "Get me a latte, will you – with soya."

"No problem," Julie smiles back as nonchalantly as she can.

What the hell is she doing? A moment of doubt hits Julie hard as soon as she sits down in the Starbucks armchair. Her fingers are shaking, she realises. They're striped with sunlight like the café tiles. A small trickle of summer has filtered through the slatted blinds to pool in front of her. If she stepped forward an inch and released her feet from their man-made heels, her wet toes would glisten warmly. Or glint like daggers. Julie feels guilt and fear lap blackly around her, stealing her sunshine.

"Fuck you, Lucy!" Julie mutters and bursts into tears.

Turning her face quickly towards the wall, away from any passing glances, Julie dabs her eyes dry with a napkin. Using her smart phone as a mirror, she tidies away the last sign of her sudden weakness, then looks up.

The light has gone and she's surrounded by suits, a gurgling espresso machine and clinking chairs. Through the glass doors, nothing but grey pavement, dark clouds and tower blocks. Even the horizon is jagged, the sky above a cold ocean. But this is the world they live in, office politics the norm, to be expected even. She's simply killing two birds with one stone: legitimate revenge on Lucy and the possibility of knocking out nasty Nick at the same time. Or using it as her chance to step in and save the day: "Let me recall them, Nick, we'll say tech gremlins deleted a paragraph from the plans, outlining the campaign's underlying twist-in-the-tale narrative bait…" So what if Nick's wife finds out about his affair through Julie's plan, his wife ought to know anyway, right?

Her scheme is minor compared to Nick's nastiness and Lucy's machinations. But Julie can hear a little voice inside whispering: "Is this really how you think now? Why do you want to work there anyway if that's what Lucy's like, and

Nick's even worse!"

By the time she gets back to her desk twenty minutes later, Julie has a letter of resignation drafted in her head.

"Good break?" Lucy grabs a coffee from Julie's cardboard tray as soon as Julie places it down.

Julie nods non-committally, but Lucy doesn't seem to notice.

"Ugh, that's sickly: cow's milk not soya!" Lucy's voice is sharp, sour, but then she looks up quickly and pulls a quirky face as if to soften her words.

Lucy's eyes are over-bright. Julie notices too how fast they dart away from her own. Simply fear of connecting? Or that Julie might look too deep and see something Lucy doesn't want her to, something that Lucy's trying to hide? Any last doubts Julie had about her planted file have gone, from the minute she stepped back into the office and the second she heard the tone in Lucy's voice. What's to stop Lucy if Julie doesn't fight back and leaves without doing anything? If Julie's wrong about Lucy, the file stays unread. Whatever happens next is in Lucy's own hands.

Coffee cup still at her lips despite the cow's milk, Lucy turns away.

Julie's laptop is closed on her desk. Does it feel warmer

than it should, as if someone's been using it? She lifts the lid, logs back in, opens her email.

A new email from Lucy stands out bold and black at the top of Julie's inbox.

'Eureka: New Branding with Edge!' The subject line of Lucy's message to the board and her team is the title from Julie's file.

Julie doesn't even open Lucy's email. Instead, she clicks on the 'new message' icon and starts to type.

"Julie, can I speak to you?" Nick summons her three hours later, ninety minutes after the board's message instructing staff to delete Lucy's 'corrupted' attachment and an hour after the security guards escorted Lucy from the building.

Julie can feel everyone's eyes on her as she walks over to his office. The past hour their whole open-plan floor has felt like a giant aquarium, glances darting from face to face, trying to suss what's going on. She shuts Nick's door gently behind her.

Nick's standing behind his desk, looking agitated. His normally smooth silver hair is sticking up in untidy spikes.

"Your resignation…"

"Yes, it feels like time to move on."

"I see. Well, um…it's not great timing here. We've had

things happen today."

"I saw Lucy leave?"

"Yes, it's awkward. I can't talk about it. But she's left us in the lurch."

"I'm sorry to hear that."

"It means there's a gap. Before I forward your email on to the board, I don't know if you've ever considered yourself in her role?"

"I..." Julie hesitates for a moment, tempted. A pay rise. The chance to get ahead. It's exactly what she'd always hoped for. And an even bigger revenge than she'd planned. Julie can't help imagining Lucy's reaction.

"Thing is," Nick moves round the desk towards Julie, resting his hand on her shoulder. She can feel his breath on her cheek. "You'd make a great team leader. And I'd welcome the chance to work more closely with you."

"Thank you," Julie steps away. "I appreciate the offer, but I don't think it's for me."

As she leaves, Julie pulls Nick's door closed with a decisive click.

Nine Green Bottles…

"Are you listening, Julie?" her sister, Claire, asks excitedly. "I want to tell you something!"

"Sure. What is it?" Julie stirs her coffee absent-mindedly, her small circles loop in time with the café fan spinning round and round above their heads.

"I'm pregnant!"

"Really? Wow!" Julie puts her spoon down. "I mean congratulations!"

"Thanks. It's probably too soon really to say, but…"

"Planned, yeah?"

"Yes. No. Kind of. Think I'm six weeks."

"Remember what cousin Tim was like as a baby? Never shut up." Julie watches closely for her sister's reaction. She feels mean challenging Claire in the same way she might if checking out a client. But Julie wants to be sure that the pregnancy is Claire's idea, not her brother-in-law's.

"You weren't an easy baby yourself! Can't you be happy for us?" Claire's reaction is immediate, natural.

"I am! Just surprised." Julie curbs her desire to sigh. She hugs her sister. Of course, Claire wants a baby, a pretty house, an adoring husband and… nothing more. Why should she want more if a family will make her happy?

Julie watches Claire tip another spoonful of sugar into her coffee. Such sickly sweetness is Claire all over, forcing everything to be frothy and saccharine-coated. Not even six-weeks pregnant and telling everyone. It seems strange to Julie that her sister would choose to see the world as a fairytale or soppy love flick. And even stranger that Claire doesn't want more excitement, more challenge, a career along with having children.

Julie smiles at the waiter. His dark hair, and the way he moves! She'd like to slip her palm between his shirt buttons and feel the muscles beneath that white cotton…

But he's on the young side and if she were looking for a new love or lust, which she definitely isn't right now, she would be after a man with the same drive that she thrives on. Not that she looks down on him being a waiter, more on the limitations that come with it. Drive, the one thing that she and her brother-in-law have in common. Julie bites her bottom lip, unhappy with where this observation is taking her. She doesn't want to like Gary, distrusts him really, but that mixture of determination, passion and devotion, someone who will totally adore her as Gary does Claire: she very much does get the attraction of that.

"Anyway," Julie stops her thoughts drifting in that direction. "Did I tell you about our latest deal? Nick reckons I've a good chance of making the board, give it a year or two."

"That's good!"

"I know, I can't quite believe it. Great bonuses last quarter too. And I might get to go to New York next month!"

"New York? Big Apple lights and shopping, huh. Won't that be a long flight though?"

"It's not too bad. Not much worse than some of my journeys over here. I need to do it if I want promotion."

"You work so hard already though."

"Yes. But I love it. Besides, it's the way it is. This is still a man's world." Julie hesitates. She wants to add more: a man and a bitch's world. But she's not sure Claire would get it. Julie's not sure she gets it herself yet. The nastiness of that world, the falseness, the betrayal.

"Yeah, of course."

No, Julie thinks, Claire wouldn't get it all. But then Claire never has, her life so softly cushioned by everyone around her. Julie doubts her sister's even listening, let alone listening well enough to pick up on the truth. New York: some chance!

It's two weeks now since Julie quit her job and she has no idea what she's going to do next. Claire has always seen her as such a high-flier, what would her sister think if she knew the reality? As Claire babbles on, Julie distances herself from her sister's actual words. She lets her own mouth switch to responding with automatic phrases while her mind bubbles over.

"Look!" Claire interrupts Julie's thoughts. "I've even dug out some of our old toys. Do you remember this?"

Julie tries to avoid the waiter's eye and ignore the other customers' glances, though she can feel them sneering as her sister pulls out a battered red kaleidoscope. Claire puts the kaleidoscope to her eye and twists. Julie looks at her, sighing inwardly. So much about her sister is childlike. Julie envies this almost as much as she's embarrassed by it. The simplicity of naivety. One turn of Claire's kaleidoscope and the whole outlook changes as beautifully as the word itself suggests, were her sister even aware that 'kalos' is Greek for 'beautiful'.

But Claire only sees the wonder of things. Julie's the one who's had to master the practicalities and the science of life. The Greek 'eidos' means 'form' and 'scopios' is 'view'. What her sister's actually holding is a tube of mirrors with an eyepiece and an object box at the opposite end. Claire's shimmering patterns are merely fragments of coloured glass, beads, tinsel, or other ant-size reflective materials that move when tapped. Diffused light and reflections are the real source of each colourful illusion. Julie's thoughts chunder: where Claire sees a pretty toy, the reality's more like a plastic ant farm in a hall of mirrors. Not so different from the world and work, only with more symmetry.

These observations are mean, Julie rebukes herself. Her sister can't help it. And Julie should never have brought her to Café Coco, particularly not right now when Julie has her own problems to sort out.

"Gosh, Claire, I'm sorry," Julie looks at her watch and pulls her 'what's life like' expression for her sister. "I'd best get back. They don't really like us taking lunch unless it's business. And I have to sweet-talk productivity and profit-margins this afternoon!"

Julie signals the waiter over as she slides a twenty pound note out of her wallet and onto the black glossed table. Once her last pay cheque is gone, she'll be down to the hovering line of her overdraft; she needs a new job.

"I'll call you in the week." Julie kisses her sister's cheek and rushes towards the door before Claire has time to register that she's leaving.

Eight Green Bottles...

"Blag it, love," Julie's dad holds out the job ad he's found.

"But I don't have library experience, never even worked in a bookstore." Julie looks at the square of newspaper, reluctant to take it. She'd rather sort out her own life.

"You were always reading as a kid. Look how much you know!"

"That's not the same thing!"

Her dad's hand is still held out, unwavering. Julie knows he's not going to give up. She grabs the piece of paper and drops it into her pocket without looking.

"It's never stopped you before!" Her dad definitely isn't letting this go. "There aren't that many jobs you haven't tried, are there?"

"Thanks a lot, Dad!"

"You could take it as a compliment. I'm proud of you, you know, even if you always do your own thing and won't take advice."

"Huh!"

"And that woman, where you were before?"

"She had to leave. Nick was hanging in there, but not looking happy. Nothing official from the board but..."

"What your mum would have called comeuppance."

"Yeah. I don't miss it."

"That's my girl! But you do need a new job."

"I know!" Julie regrets her sharpness almost as soon as she's spoken. Her dad might be bull-in-a-china-shop belligerent at times but at least he cares.

"Give it a try. If you don't get it, nothing lost."

"I guess."

"If you get it but don't like it, you can always leave."

"Maybe." His advice is sound, Julie thinks, though there's no way she's going to admit that.

"Like you have before." Her dad winks, his serious face relaxing at last into a smile, a good sign that he's finished with the topic, and they can move onto something lighter.

"Ouch!" Julie jabs back, with a laugh. "That got me!"

"Did you see that new programme…"

As they settle into chatting about comfortably insignificant things, Julie's fingers play with the crinkled ad in her pocket. Strictly speaking, she isn't qualified. But it's true she loves books and has mastered confidence the hard way. There are plenty of things to smooth over any shortfall in experience. And it would definitely help her finances, even if only as a stop-gap.

Seven Green Bottles...

He called, Julie smiles, the gorgeous guy from the library called her. Who'd have thought being able to tell her Whitman from her Dickinson would not only land her a job that she enjoys but also a hot date, and in just a few weeks! Her dad's right, blagging is her ultimate skill, though only because she quickly learns what she doesn't know.

> *"Hope" is the thing with feathers –*
> *That perches in the soul...*

Julie isn't that convinced about poetry, even Emily Dickinson's. But she can definitely feel a warm fluttering inside anticipating her evening with Dan. His short dark hair, those almost amber eyes, the way their fingers brushed over his copy of *Mountains of the Mind*. She had to scan it twice!

She isn't sure his suggestion of climbing is an ideal date though. It sounds rather unsexily sweaty, and unfamiliar territory, not the safest for presenting herself in the best light.

"Am I really doing this?" Julie thinks as she follows the instructor's demonstration for putting on her harness. She's had to tie her hair back and the orange helmet makes her feel like a workman preparing to enter a construction site, only instead of boots, she's had to force her feet into tiny leather shoes that pinch.

Still, she's here now. And so is Dan. Although he's joked that he's not climbed in a while, he's looking more than good in the kit. Very toned and muscular in fact. Julie forces her mind quickly back to the instructor's words. How to tie a double figure-of-eight and stopper knot, maintaining a firm stance, different harnesses, caribiners and belay devices. The physics of gravity, counterweight and safety. Then the actual climbing.

Julie finds it harder than it looks, much harder, particularly the final route she's chosen. Sheer fear and a sickness that's close to panic almost stop her several times. Bolstered by her first, easier, climbs and Dan shouting, "Go on, you can do it," she'd been determined to try the next grade up, not realising quite how much this would challenge her. But she can't back out now, not without looking wimpish. She knows that Dan's below, watching.

She moves slowly upwards, hand after foot after hand. Some holds aren't too bad. Others little more than small plastic wedges. She stretches out, bends body and limbs at awkward angles, tries to place feet and grip in a way that fits each hold yet feels secure. Then she balances the rest of her body around this, before moving on again.

By the time she reaches the top, Julie's exhausted. But as she places her second hand on the last hold, exhilaration rushes through her. She's done it!

"Great stuff!" Julie hears Dan shout. Is there as much excitement in his voice as she's feeling now? If he hasn't been put off by her slow clumsiness and clammy fringe…

"Sit back," the instructor calls.

She lets go of the top hold and swings out from the wall, waiting for him to lower her. The first thing she's going to do when she reaches the ground again is get this bloody helmet off, then shake out her hair.

After climbing, pizza. Despite Julie's initial gut feeling that her stomach won't take it, she's surprised to find that she's starving. A whole 16-inch Hawaiian and a bottle of Shiraz later, her and Dan's legs and fingers have brushed several times. His eyes are sparkling. She suspects hers must be too.

Dan drives her home. Five minutes and they're back at hers. Dan leans over to say goodbye; they kiss.

The kiss is long, slow, luxurious. Even Dan's breath triggers gentle tingles across her skin, unhooking every clenched muscle inside her. She feels his fingers brush her cheek, the soft flurry of air around them, then the slow, fast, fast, slow press of his presence as they kiss again. And again.

When they finally pull apart, Julie considers asking him in. But something stops her. It's not a lack of wanting. Julie wants this, him, as much, if not more, than she's wanted any man before. But she also needs it to be right, in a way that mostly hasn't bothered her in the past. Dan isn't just some guy. Already, she cares what he thinks of her. The potential for this to be something great is balanced only by the amount it's going to hurt if it doesn't work out.

"Call me?" she asks, exactly at the moment that he says the same.

They both laugh, and she tucks a stray hair behind her ear. Before she closes the car door, she turns back to look at him.

"Tomorrow." He smiles.

She smiles back and feels his eyes watching her as she walks to her flat door, then opens it. Julie turns to wave, he waves back and pulls away.

They're mundane details, everyday actions and gestures, Julie thinks as she steps inside. But even before she's taken off her coat, her mobile has bleeped with a new text.

Great night. We should do it again – soon! Dan x

Julie smiles. Right now, caring feels good, important even, whatever risk or pain might come later.

Do you like Thai? Dan x

How was work? What about a walk instead of climbing? xx

Day follows night follows day. Text follows text follows phone call. Kiss follows kiss leads to… A soul full of feathers and a heart that "sings the tune without the words," Julie thinks, humming as she showers, cuts her toast, hangs the tea towel to dry, flicks through ads, plumps up cushions…

Miss you. Stay over next time? Xx

Six Green Bottles...

"What do you mean a crash?" Julie's tone is shrill. Her mobile's shaking and her other hand's clenched so tightly that her nails leave crescent marks on her palm.

"What do you mean, Claire?" Julie repeats, hearing her own voice as if it were someone else's, its pitch higher and higher with each question. She's trying to understand what her sister's saying. But instead of Claire's words making more sense, Julie feels further and further out of control of their meaning.

"Dad?"

"Yes, a concrete bridge. Instant, they said."

"Where? When? What are the police doing?"

"I don't know. It's so muddled, Julie. I couldn't take it all in." Claire's speaking so quietly that her sister can barely hear her over the sound of their combined breathing, the words distorted as if underwater.

"And the funeral, we need to sort the funeral. Will there be an inquest?"

"I don't know, I, um..."

Julie hears a crackling and then it's Gary on the line, alternating between confused non-answers and calming sureness. The pitch of Julie's speech drops but it's still not normal. It's as if she's at work taking control of a potential disaster but, instead of hearing the questions in her head, she's listening to herself speaking from the other side of a window.

After the phone call, Julie's like a fish flapping in a net: she flits around the room, thoughts thrashing, then stops, rock-stunned and gills throbbing.

She starts to distract herself with work emails. But the words are like cars in rush-hour traffic, merging into one dense flow without clarity or meaning. One second, she's typing a colleague's name or a book title, and then she's back reliving her last conversation with her dad or imagining his Fiesta in a mangled tangle of metal and bricks.

Julie paces, sits, paces. She breaks a vase banging it down too hard, then more pacing, sitting, pacing. Finally, she phones Dan at work. She knows it's too soon for her to let her guard down with him, too soon for this kind of trust but his initial tone of frustration at her flustered interruption is quickly replaced by decisive concern. He's at her flat within fifteen minutes, arms around her, not saying anything, simply listening as she sobs.

Later, she tells Dan that though this brought them closer, she thinks that was the day that she began to lose her sister as well as her dad. Claire and she speak almost daily on the phone. But the inquest, the funeral arrangements, even Claire's birthing plan are like touching and speaking with her sister through layers of cling film. It's Gary who organises, Gary she talks to when she tries to make sense of what happened, Gary who asks how she's coping. When Claire doesn't even manage to come to the inquest with Julie, it's like a thousand bottles exploding into sharp fragments of anger and betrayal. And loneliness. Julie's never needed to be not-alone in the way she does now.

The coroner's verdict should bring closure. But it doesn't. 'Accidental death' feels like a mockery. Few things in life are truly accidental, Julie thinks. Always one thing that provokes another – a logic, a choice, a reason. If Dad hadn't been there at that point, going to wherever it was that he was going… Where was he going? It seems inconceivable that nobody should know. It can't even have been two days since she last saw him, and he'd not said anything. But then, why would he? The shops, barbers maybe, an impromptu visit to a friend… And the word 'accidental', labelling his death like any small mistake. As if it were a typo, a blip, an insignificant slip, she can't, won't, bear to have it dismissed that way. It matters because he mattered, which means all the unanswered questions matter too.

Or perhaps she's kidding herself. Maybe the word and

her questions only matter because 'accidental' suggests something that could have been prevented, changed, brought to a different outcome. And this can't, not now anyway.

When she isn't busy with work, Julie occupies herself by doodling on her notepad. Then she buys a sketchbook on a whim that seems to come from somewhere beyond her usual rational thinking. Julie remembers her mum painting when they were small, then pencil sketches when she and Dad moved onto the boat. Small unfinished snatches of canal life. Unfinished had been Mum all over, full of ideas and imagination but never able to stick with them long enough to see them through. Completing things had always been Dad's forte.

Dad hadn't been one for keeping things though. Sorting the narrowboat ready for sale, she doesn't find any of Mum's sketches, nor in his lock-up. But she is surprised by a document wallet of pictures and paper stowed next to an old black Bible. Inside the book's cover, a family tree: their family tree; Julie recognises her and Claire's names, Granny Compton, Uncle Len. Mostly her mum's handwriting. But bits added here and there in her dad's hand: towns, dates, job details. There are letters to relatives with her mum's signature, and old photos too. Julie can feel tears in her eyes at the beaming, almost besotted, smiles on her parents' strangely young faces.

Julie remembers how her dad used to sing 'Twinkle, Twinkle Little Star.' And the stories he made up! His versions of the classic fairy tales from playschool. Then, as she got older, different, more striking ones. Her favourite was 'The Cello Woman'. Her dad wouldn't say where his story came from. Sometimes he recalled it as a childhood memory from before he was old enough to register details clearly. Other times it was a half-overheard anecdote that he must have picked up while travelling, before he met her mum. The story was slightly different on every retelling but the central elements clear and vivid.

"There was once a young widow as beautiful as she was sad. After her husband's death, this woman carried his cello case with her everywhere she went. The black curves were cumbersome, awkward, nudging and bruising those who brushed past as she queued at the butcher's, the grocer's, the post office… People muttered around her, louder and louder, but still she carried this with her and no one dared to confront her.

"Then, one day, a little boy stopped to stroke the case's curves, to ask if he might see it, touch it, play. The woman nodded sadly and opened the case.

"A sea of black feathers poured out, but no instrument. Sold to pay her rent, there was no cello. So, saddened by the woman's face, the little boy plucked the absent cello's strings. The young widow saw then how the empty case's echoes of her husband's music had hollowed the world and turned her life to dead wood. She took the case home and never brought it out again. But, each day, she wrote a short love note to her husband and placed it inside until the case fluttered with paper butterflies…"

The story's too sad for Julie to remember without crying. The voice that retells it in her head isn't right either. It's her dad's but not her dad's. Her emotions feel the same in memory, but already she can only replay his exact intonations in snatches. The rest's like a faulty recording, distorted by white noise.

Julie stuffs photos and letters back into the wallet. Funny that her mum had put so much effort into this, that her dad had kept it, and that Julie didn't know about it. Except, of course, it isn't really. Her parents had their own lives, sides to their personalities that she'd never seen. Julie knows this logically, emotionally less so until now. It's like being left with the remains of two strangers while she's desperately scrabbling for something solid and familiar to hold onto.

Julie puts Bible and document wallet in a box, and

concentrates on emptying the boat. She black bags her dad's clothes as quickly and mechanically as she can to avoid being ambushed by any memories. But they still catch her, hiding in the most unexpected things. The fork her dad had bent to a makeshift corkscrew, the chipped wood where he dropped a saucepan, the last mug Mum bought him…

It's no good. Julie sighs. Everything she touches is a memory. And she wants to remember, but she wants to remember with control. She wants to relive her mum and dad in their last few months together before Mum's cancer. She wants to hold onto those daily moments of happiness that no one thinks to photograph. Instead, what she recollects most is the time that she dropped by unexpectedly while Mum was in hospital and found her dad with painkillers lined up on the table. Next to empty squashed cardboard and plastic packets, the small heap of pills.

He'd sworn he wasn't thinking of doing anything stupid, simply clearing her mum's clutter. But the way his hand shook when he brushed them into a bin bag. The pain and futility in his eyes. Julie shivers recalling it, feeling that lack inside herself too. If only there'd been an eye witness to the crash. She can't help thinking that certainty would make his death easier to deal with. Someone who'd seen a cat leap across the road and her dad swerving. Someone who'd been distracted by the same thing. Someone with something that made sense of losing him.

Catching Julie in the middle of drawing, Dan teases the details from her memory-sketch of her dad's stricken face.

"You're tired." Dan squeezes her hand. "And that's distorting things."

"You think?"

"Yes. If your dad had intended to crash, the police would have found something."

"He missed Mum a lot."

"But he dealt with it. What you saw then was most likely fear, suddenly realising how ill she was. Even if the thought of doing something crossed his mind momentarily, he wasn't that sort of man."

"He was very down to earth and get on with life."

"His shaking was likely anger or frustration."

"He was angry then, angry that he couldn't save her."

"Exactly. Anger not despair. And that was then. If there'd been something else recently, his friends would have noticed. We would too. But there wasn't."

"I guess."

"Look how stoked he was when you started at the library, Claire's pregnancy, his next trip up north."

Julie remembers. Only the week before his death, her dad hadn't stopped wittering about his plans to tour Burton's breweries while catching up with his mates in Hanley. She smiles. Dan is right, they've always been a family that got on with things, like Dad's 'Cello Woman'. Telling herself this, Julie throws herself into the funeral arrangements, library projects and preparing for Claire's baby just as her dad had thrown himself into his friends, hobbies, plans.

Five Green Bottles…

"Julianna? You're calling her Julianna?"

Already shocked by the pleasant warmth of her niece in her arms, Julie can't believe the joy that she feels at the thought of having this cute little being named after her! The emotion surprises her as it has done every day since her niece's birth. 'Cute' is not a word made for Julie's tongue. As for tears, their wetness blurring her vision and smudging her make-up, she blinks them away.

"I know it's soppy. But you'll be her godmother as well as her auntie."

"I… That's wonderful."

"You don't mind, do you?"

"Of course not! I'm surprised that's all. But it's lovely, thank you."

Unsure what more to say, Julie smiles at Dan across the nursery as she reaches across to grip her sister's hand. Claire squeezes hers back and, for a moment, it's like everything that's real and important is there in that room, with rainbows stretched across the walls and musical fishes swimming through sunlight above Ju's cot.

Then Claire breaks away to twist the handle on the musical box which Julie has bought for the baby. Claire opens the lid. They watch the fairy inside twirl. After Julie bought it, she worried the present might be too impractical next to baby clothes and rattles. But she was the baby's aunt and she wanted to get something special, something Claire and Gary wouldn't buy themselves, something her niece might keep.

As Claire relaxes into motherhood, Julie finds herself relaxing into her own life. She stops caring about promotion and looking at other jobs online. Instead, she enjoys spending longer evenings with Dan, takes more walks in the park with Ju and Claire, or rocks Ju in her arms while her sister sleeps and Gary cooks their tea.

Doesn't she realise then that this is too good to be true? Doesn't she notice how pale and tired Claire is? Yes, Julie tells herself later, but that's to be expected with a young baby, isn't it? That's why she jokes with Claire about sleep deprivation, why Julie and Gary get on with things so that Claire can get some rest, why Auntie Julie is always on hand even before Claire or Gary need anything for Ju.

"Can't I come round earlier?" Dan questions one afternoon on the phone.

"I won't be there."

"Again?"

"Don't be like that. I'll be back soon as Ju's down for

the night."

"Would you rather I not bother?"

"It's not that, Dan, don't get in a mood. Claire and Gary need my help."

"I don't want to eat late though, not with work tomorrow!"

"I won't be too late, promise."

"That's what you said last time," Dan's voice is still grumpy but she can hear his barbed tone settling into rough-edged acceptance.

"Let yourself in, and I'll get Indian on my way back."

"Chicken vindaloo and naan."

"And a nargis kebab. I'll make it up to you, promise."

"You'd better," Dan's gruffness takes on a lighter tinge, and their goodbyes fall naturally into a synchronistic chorus.

"It's good to feel useful," Julie confides later, snuggling against Dan's chest. "I'm sure Ju almost smiled today. They say babies don't this early, but I'm sure she did."

"You're besotted!" Dan laughs, smoothing Julie's hair away from her face.

"I know. It's so strange after all that's happened." Julie kisses his hand then grips it in her own. "The pain's still there, but it's like I know how Mum and Dad would feel. They can't hold Ju, but I can. I can sense Dad watching us, and sometimes when I'm talking, it's as if it's Mum's words; I never realised that before."

"She must have been a wonderful woman."

"Yes. And Dad was great too," Julie rubs her head gently against Dan's shoulder. "You only got to see a fraction of him. When we were small, he used to take me to the park or let me help him with the car while Mum took Claire to dance class. He'd get me ice cream. A whippy with a chocolate flake. Our treat."

"Special moments. And your dad's sweet tooth!" Dan kisses her forehead.

"Yeah, I'm glad you got to meet him. He liked you: his kind of man. I don't think he or Mum were ever sure what to make of Gary, me neither you know, for all that Claire adores him. But then I haven't always been sure what to make of Claire."

"No?"

"Withdrawn, funny moods. I think she was bullied at school."

"Yeah?"

"She never said. But I heard things. Maybe I should have done something."

"How old were you?"

"Six, seven maybe."

"What could you have done?"

"Told her to stick up for herself. Shown her how to."

"Judo Julie and the art of being strong!" Dan laughs gently. "Seriously though, she was what...nine or ten? And you were six. Not quite ready to rule the world and shoulder your sister's problems, whatever caused them."

"Easy for you to say with your family."

"We have our screw-ups too, you know. My nan was seriously coco loco! And Claire has Gary and Ju now."

"That's true. I think Mum and Dad always worried Gary was a bit aloof, not the stick-around type. But the way he helped to organise the funeral. Perfect for Dad. Practical like Dad too."

"Don't forget my expert steering!"

"Yes, we would have been lost without you."

"We?"

"Okay, me. I would have been lost without you."

"Good that I'm the stick-around type then. Assuming you want me to?"

"Of course, though you could stop leaving wet towels on my floor."

"If you stop writing on my newspaper."

"The newspaper you don't even read!"

"I do read it. But not the boring sections!"

"Hmm… I guess we can work on these. Might even get you to master the perfect cup of coffee!"

Smiling, Julie turns to face him. Her lips kissing slowly upwards from chin to mouth, she strokes her fingers through his dark chest hair, then pulls his body down on hers.

Later, nuzzling her head against his neck, Julie curls her fingers in and out of his hair again as if weaving dreams from them. She breathes in his scent, feels his muscled warmth sturdy and firm behind her.

Four Green Bottles…

"Do you think we might have a baby, maybe, one day?"

Cuddled up next to Dan on the sofa, the words are said before Julie realises she's saying them. She hears Dan suck in his breath and her stomach clenches. She's said the wrong thing. It's too soon, too daft. She should have kept her mouth shut, it's not like she's ever been mum-material anyway.

Then Dan breathes out again slowly and looks at her.

"I hadn't thought about it. But seeing you with Ju, and what you said the other night… you'd make a great mum, so I'd say it's likely."

Julie tries out the shape of his words in her mind, slowly registering their import. Then doubt, and her heart beating faster.

"Likely me with a baby? Or me with your baby."

"Do you need to ask?"

"No." Julie replies slowly. "But tell me anyway."

"Us, with our baby, when the time's right."

"Of course. Not now. Not when life's so full-on. But later."

Julie's fingers trace the contours of Dan's face, his forehead, the hollows around his brown eyes, butterfly touches across his cheeks. Her lips press his, gently biting his lip. Releasing him from this kiss, she takes his left hand, places it on her breast and asks, "This, what you said earlier, is that you making some kind of commitment?"

"Depends...is that your hand making my kind of commitment?" Dan raises his eyebrow quizzically and bends forwards to brush his lips across her nipple.

"Hey, that's not fair! I asked first!" Julie laughs.

"Yes, then. Least, so long as your answer's yes."

"Aren't you meant to be down on bended knee?"

"Down on something," Dan laughs, then whispers in her ear, "So, Julie Faulkner, will you marry me?"

He pulls away from her, the laughter gone from his face as he stares into her eyes and repeats the question louder.

Julie's answer is as quick and as sure as any she's ever given. As they kiss, longer, slower, deeper than before, it's like diving into a tropical pool; every cell in her body shimmers with this warm glistening.

Three Green Bottles…

"We need to talk!" Julie's tone is quiet but curt.

Gary jumps back from straightening Ju's blanket as she sleeps cradled in Julie's arms.

Julie glances over at her sister, curled up asleep in the armchair. Claire's head has lolled against the chair's arm at the same awkward angle as Ju's is against Julie's arm. An open, completely defenceless position, Julie thinks, pain and anger battling inside her.

"Not in here," she snarls slightly. "In the kitchen. When I've put Ju down."

Julie lays her niece in the cot, tipping Ju slightly as she loosens her arms from underneath. Ju sighs, then settles back into her soft baby-breathing.

"Well, that was a mammoth job, Auntie Julie," Gary smiles at Julie, and hands her a mug of coffee.

"Don't!" Julie scowls as she clunks the mug down on the kitchen table. Weak, over-creamy, coffee jolts across the cloth. "Who's that woman you were down town with last week?"

"What woman?" Gary's reply is quick, but not so quick that Julie doesn't see panic flash across his face. She has seen guilt and shame before, read the tell-tale signs in clients who lie for a living. Gary isn't even near their league. But none of them mattered as much as this.

"You bastard. My sister's in there knackered out from looking after your daughter, while you're off snogging some other bitch and fuck knows what else!"

"No!"

"Yes! Don't lie to me. I saw you!"

"I…it…" Gary dabs a dishcloth at the milky brown spillage from Julie's coffee, avoiding her eyes. "It's not like that, really it's not, Julie." He slumps onto one of the kitchen chairs and looks up at her with pleading eyes. "Let me explain."

"Go on then," Julie straightens her back, refusing to look at him or sit down at his level. "Not that I can see anything explaining that!"

"No, you're right; it was wrong, very wrong. But it's not what you think."

"What is it then? A goodbye kiss for your sister!"

"No, I mean, it's not an affair, not even a real kiss. Karen's leaving do, she'd had a bit too much to drink and… Please, Julie, it was one stupid, drunken, half-kiss, something that happened before I realised it was happening. I love Claire. Don't tell her."

"Why on earth wouldn't I tell her, you bastard?" Julie

repeats, turning her back on him. She throws her coffee into the sink.

"You can't tell her. It was a one-off, a mistake. Things have been hard at work, and the lack of sleep with Ju… I wasn't thinking or I'd have stopped it quicker."

"If it ever, ever happens again…" Julie glares at Gary and bangs her mug down against the sink again, breaking the handle. "Then I'm telling her. And don't think I won't. I'm watching you. Everywhere and anywhere. I'll know and I will tell her!"

Two Green Bottles...

"I think you'd best go." Claire's face is pale but determined as she stares at her sister.

"But why? What's the matter?" Julie stares back, stunned by Claire's abrupt tone. Her sister's expression isn't one Julie's seen before, not on her sister, not at work, a mixture of something like terror and hatred. Her sister's arms are full of blue curtains; a trail of satin and lining drags behind her, white hooks clattering faintly.

"I don't think we need your help any more, thank you." As Claire pushes her towards the door, Julie hears several hooks crack under her feet.

Before she can think to stand her ground or push back, Julie finds herself outside. The kitchen door is slammed behind her. Then, the noise of Claire turning the key and the scrape of the bolt.

"But Claire!" Julie pounds her fists on the door. "Let me in, Claire!"

But her sister doesn't answer. Julie has never seen her like this, can't believe the strength with which Claire forced her to the door. And now she can hear Ju crying.

"Claire!"

But Claire doesn't answer. Julie tries the door handle

again. Still locked. She puts her ear to the door: Ju's cries, cars in the street, next door's cat on the gravel, but no sound of Claire.

Julie tries the front door. It's locked too. She bends her ear to the letter box but all she can hear is Ju crying.

Julie feels in her pocket for her mobile to ring Dan or Gary. But her handbag's still inside, and with it her phone.

The neighbours!

Mumbling about locking herself out while Claire's sleeping, Julie uses Frank's land-line next-door to call Gary, grateful that his firm's number is memorably simple. As she taps the buttons, Frank natters about the council, the sycamore trees, the litter in the street.

"Sorry, Frank," she nods as she hears her brother-in-law pick up and turns away from the old man.

"Gary, it's Julie. Claire's locked me out the house and Ju's crying. I don't know what to do, I'm not sure what's wrong. I've never seen her like this!"

"Can't it wait? I'm in a meeting." Gary sounds exasperated.

"No, Gary." Julie hears her own voice shrilling. "I don't think it can wait. You need to come now!"

One Green Bottle…

"Julie, are you awake?" Dan sits on the edge of the double bed beside Julie and rests a hand on her duvet-wrapped body. "That was Phil asking how you are. And if you're well enough to come back to work yet?"

Huddled in the duvet's thick protective pelt, Julie merely grunts as she has done every morning for the past two weeks.

"Can I get you a coffee before I leave? Or open the curtains?"

"No!"

"Are you sure?"

"I said, didn't I?"

"It might help to get back into routine."

"Not now. Let me sleep."

"A friend's given me a website link. He lost his second to cot death. He said talking to others helped his wife."

Julie doesn't reply. Even Dan's words seem to come in slow motion, like a battering of rain and twigs against glass. There's a comfort in the way they keep coming though. A rhythm as certain as her own heartbeat. As regular as Ju's breathing in her arms. The thought's another shock that pierces through the numbness.

Julie presses her face deeper into her pillow before Dan can see her tears. First Mum, then Dad, and now Ju. The pain swells and ebbs but, when it comes, it twists her body to a rope. On top of it all, to find out too that her sister thinks she's having an affair with Gary. Julie could strangle her. As if Gary would ever be her sort, even if he weren't her brother in law, even if she weren't with Dan. The brittle irony too, when she'd seen Gary with that woman and tried to protect Claire. If that isn't proof of how loopy her sister has gone!

At first, she was tempted to confront Gary again, scared that might be part of what had driven Claire crazy. But at Ju's graveside, his crying was uncontrollable. His trousers were all saggy, pulled into pleats at the waist; he'd clearly lost a lot of weight and had deep hollows of tiredness around his eyes as well as a straggly beard. At the end of the funeral, he tried to go to Claire, but she pushed him away.

When Julie went across to him afterwards, he simply sobbed. "I don't understand. I love her. I didn't do anything, why won't she talk to me, Julie?"

Julie couldn't answer; her sister refused to see anyone. Julie looked into Gary's eyes and saw nothing but confusion and shadows. Everything about him was more broken than the kaleidoscope on Ju's floor that day. After all the liars and players that she'd worked with, Julie was pretty damn sure that Gary wasn't hiding anything.

Later, processing her sister's lack of trust, Julie's shocked by how little Claire knows her. Also, how little she knows Claire, not to realise her sister could doubt her in that way, illness or no illness. Guilt shudders through Julie. That she didn't notice how Claire was struggling, even before Ju's death. Black as Julie feels now, Ju wasn't her daughter. Julie can't eat, can barely breathe without feeling sick, every thought drags her back to this churning hollowness. If this is how she feels, what must Claire be going through?

"It's not your fault, you know. It will get easier," Dan says this so softly that she can barely make out the words. "Not better, but easier, I promise."

He leans over, drawing back the top of the duvet to kiss her. She twitches her face away so that his lips brush her cheek instead of her mouth. The only thing worse than Claire and Ju is having to deal with the pain and helplessness on Dan's face. She hears him sigh.

"I'll see you later. Love you."

Julie listens as the bedroom door hinges creak, then the heavy click and clunk of the front door closing.

"Love you too," she whispers. Her words hang in the air behind Dan like the mist of warm breath on a cold winter's morning. She shouldn't have snapped, it wasn't his fault. And being left here alone feels desolate. She will get up soon, sort the flat, tackle her email, take control.

Exhaustion is a relief though. No thoughts, no energy for feelings. Sleep. Peace. Release. A few more hours in bed to shake the tiredness and freshen her mind, then she'll ring Phil.

Julie buries her head back under the duvet, and breathes in the scent of lavender, the same scent as Ju's bubble bath, or Ju's clothes fresh from the laundry, minus that smell of warm, talced baby. She starts to cry again, remembering the same smell in Ju's room on the day she died, people flustering around and plastic kaleidoscope shapes in a scattered glittering across the floor.

The jewellery box Julie bought for Ju is lying upside down beside Ju's cot, a silver locket spilling from it. One velour cushion pokes out under the bottom drawer of Ju's changing table, bulging with creased baby clothes. The box is wedged open but no music's playing.

Pushing the drawer in, Julie finds the jewellery-box fairy and a cracked end of red kaleidoscope. Out of its box, the tiny fairy is stiff, snapped at the knees. Julie picks the figure up and holds it tight in her fist. She recalls the moment when Claire told her Ju's name, music and smiles flowing around them. Julie's cheeks are wet with tears. She wipes them away and looks up at the room's blinded window, the subdued wattage of the up-lighter casting the mobile's fish as stilled monsters on the wall.

On the landing, a policeman, or someone from the ambulance, is talking to Claire. Her sister's face is pale and ghostly, cocooned in a shroud-like blanket. Beside her, Gary's expression is contorted in anguish. Julie watches as they lead Claire away.

No! Julie twists her thoughts from this memory and thumps her pillow. Her bedside lamp crashes to the floor. A large petal of cream ceramic falls away from the spherical base. For several minutes, Julie stares at the hole in the hollow ball, the unvarnished dark cave inside. Then she picks up the lamp and cracked fragment. As she places them on the bedside table, her foot knocks against the edge of a box wedged under the bed.

It's the box with her dad's things. Julie reaches in, pulls out the leather Bible and measures its weight in her hand. She's not a believer, nothing so stupid, but the solidity of the book is somehow reassuring. She opens the cover and traces her mum's family tree with her fingers, its pattern like a piece of lace or a part-finished sketch. Emma, James, John, Millicent, Henry, Victoria: so many people.

But are they a symbol of endurance or a reminder of the futility of life? Julie runs her finger across Claire's name, the page empty beneath it. An ink tree with no substance, branching away to nothing. What family does Julie have really? A sister she can't see and a blank space where Ju's name should be. Julie grabs the Bible and lifts the corner of several pages to tear them out…then stops. The tissue-thin paper is mottled with translucent patches from her tears. She drops the Bible. As it falls, a picture of her mum and dad's wedding flies out, drifting to the dark floor beneath the bed.

The photo lies there, face-down. Julie doesn't want to move but she forces herself to reach out and pick it up. It's not like she can sleep anyway, no matter how much she needs to. If she has to stay awake, keeping busy means less chance for thoughts to take over. Besides, it's not right to leave her parents face-down like that, even if it's only a picture. Julie owes them more, and she can't risk losing the photo, especially not through her own carelessness.

Julie lifts the box lid and slips the picture in. Her hand brushes against leather, a different leather to the Bible: softer, suede. She picks up the mottled notebook, expecting to find it empty, something she'd forgotten to throw away in the rush of clearing out Dad's boat. Instead, page after page of her dad's spidery writing, dense and compact. She reads a few sentences.

…Wendy in a violet dress I've not seen before. It glimmered like our lake in summer sunlight. Our foxtrot was slow. I think it was the band, but she says it's us, the inevitability of age. Our feet still knew the steps though!

Her mum and dad's life together in the year before her mum's death. No hint of the cancer, her dad prosaic and practical, but warmth and love in each sentence. It feels wrong to read something so private, yet…his preoccupations and feelings laid out, and neatly dated.

Julie hesitates, her hand shaking slightly at the thought that's occurred to her. Then she flicks to the back, the last few pages, the week before his accident.

No Green Bottles Standing on the Wall but if One Mossed Wall Should Accidentally Fall

…Sudden sunshine today. Hope it stays clear for the weekend. Mike reckons he's found some new brewery. We'll see. If not, The Lord Burton and Bass Pale Ale will do me. Must get a new holdall.

Her dad's last sentences are as prosaic as the rest of his journal, Julie thinks, drying her tears. She's had to read the notebook over several weeks. The first time she tried, she hunched up into a ball and cried until every muscle in her body ached. Even the matter-of-fact style was characteristic of her dad and his daily routine, evoking many small reminders of him. The hardest part was his sentimental joy at Claire's news that she was pregnant. Julie read this section once, and only once, guiltily glad that never getting to hold his grand-daughter also meant that her dad hadn't had to suffer losing her.

As she closes the journal, Julie wonders if she'll ever get to share it with anyone other than Dan. Would their dad's words help Claire or make things worse? At least Claire's refusal to see or speak to anyone means Julie doesn't have to make a decision about whether to show her the notebook.

That night, instead of dreaming about her niece or

Claire, Julie finds herself in the Fiesta beside her dad. They're careering towards a brick wall. She hears crying in the back and turns round, expecting to see Ju. Instead, there's an open cello case on the back seat, lined with red petals.

Julie turns to ask her dad about it. But now her dad's lying in the road, lopsided. A young woman in a long black dress is in the driver's seat beside Julie. And the wall that would have stopped their car slides backwards, away from them. Julie turns again to her dad. Instead of lying still, broken, his hands are straightening out his spine. He raises his head from the tarmac, looks at Julie and smiles. Reflected in the windscreen, her own smile and her mum's smiling face beside her.

The next morning, Julie places her dad's notebook back into the box and takes out a small snap of her parents' wedding. She fits it into her dad's old business card holder so that she can carry it in her pocket.

One Green Bottle…

"It can't be!" Julie closes her eyes, then looks again at the pregnancy strip. A blue line. She shakes the white plastic, the line is still there.

Julie rests her hand on her stomach. She doesn't feel any different. A little extra weight maybe but she's been trying not to acknowledge that. Besides, it isn't that much, only what she'd put down to bouts of comfort eating and being less active.

Julie reaches for the box and reads the instructions again. Yes, a blue line in the window is definitely pregnant. She sits down on the edge of the bath, trembling slightly.

She can't believe it's possible. It's not as if she and Dan have been at it like rabbits, though it has been good getting that lust back again recently. Julie licks her lip. She thought they'd been careful but…

When exactly was her last period? Before Dan's birthday, after swimming with Mel, before she had to buy some new skirts for work, so that would be six to eight weeks. It hasn't really been that long, has it?

Julie still can't quite believe it, knows Dan won't believe it either. Her tensed muscles soften and she smiles as she imagines telling Dan. His shock, surprise, then delight. She recalls the warmth in his eyes when he proposed, how light spread across his face, what he said when she mentioned babies. He will be delighted, won't he? A slight doubt starts to scratch at her. Later is what they agreed, when the timing was right. What if he doesn't want it? What if he reacts as Tom did?

Julie starts to shiver. She can't go through that again. Not now. Not after all that's happened. Not after Ju. Ju! A new, different, wave of shock clenches Julie. Even if Dan's happy, how on earth is she going to tell Claire? The place where her sister has ended up is so sterile and eerie. Glad though she is that Claire will let her visit now, Julie barely knows what to say. The only moments when Claire's face doesn't look lifeless are when it's pain-stricken, and mostly Claire doesn't even seem to register Julie's presence. It makes Julie both sad and angry that Claire should be there, like that. Give it time, the doctors keep saying, but there's only so much time available.

Julie was practically the first to hear when Claire was pregnant with Ju. But Julie has no one to share the news with other than Dan: not Mum, not Dad. And, if she tells Dan and he isn't happy…

The butterflies dancing inside Julie are now a swarm of black beetles. She's going to be sick. Julie rushes to the toilet, heaving with phantom vomiting. Her throat is knotted, she can barely swallow. Hyperventilating, Julie pulls her mobile from her pocket.

"Dan!" She starts to cry. "I can't breathe. It's all wrong, you'll be shocked and Claire will hate me!"

Julie's already much calmer by the time Dan arrives, but, having called him in such a panic and unsure of his reaction, she lets him rock her in his arms as she shows him the test strip. His body is warm around her against the cold of their bathroom tiles, their pattern of black and white diamonds splashed with sparkling fragments of sunlight reflected by the metal fittings.

"You're sure you're okay with this?" Julie plays with Dan's fingers, her hand so small beside his.

"Yes. This is what we wanted, right?"

"Of course. It's just that when we talked...well, that was then, and later, not now..."

"What do you mean?" The loud sharpness of Dan's voice startles Julie. His usually molten eyes are hard as marble.

"The timing. After Ju..."

"What are you saying, Julie? Not abortion. Don't tell me you even thought that!"

"Of course not!" Julie's shouting too now, and shaking.

She starts to cry.

"Oh, God, I'm sorry." Dan's arms are around Julie again. "I over-reacted. Stuff, you know, from the past."

"The past." Still stunned, Julie echoes his words numbly, trying not to think her of own past.

"The timing sucks," Dan strokes her hair, his eyes warm and molten again. "But we'll manage."

Julie nods. Inside though, she's a knot of clenched muscles. She's delighted about the baby, worried and delighted, but if this is how Dan feels about abortion, how would he react if he knew about her and Tom?

"How many weeks do you think you are?"

"I don't know," Julie forces herself to focus on Dan's words instead of her jagged thoughts. "I'm not sure how late I am. Didn't realise I'd stopped marking the dates in my diary."

"I reckon it was that night I cooked curry. Super chef, super sperm!" Dan kisses the back of her neck.

"Behave!"

"Me? I'm always behaving!" Dan chuckles sheepishly.

"Typical arrogant man!" Julie retorts automatically, her thoughts still churning. She stands up, steadying herself against the bathroom sink. "Bloody crying! I need to tidy my face."

"Sure." Dan smiles.

After he's gone, Julie stares at her reflection in the mirror. It's her but it's not her. Eyes, hair colour, the tilt of her lips all the same as eighteen months ago, but inside: it's as if she's her sister's ruddy kaleidoscope. Only, instead of containing beads and jewels that can be twisted into beautiful patterns, she rattles with the glass fragments of a hundred broken bottles reflected in a hundred broken ways. Pieced back together, some of those slivers were her and Tom.

Two Green Bottles...

"There's something I have to tell you." Julie tries to keep her tone light as she clears her and Dan's dinner plates from the table, but she feels like every muscle in her body has been pulled tight. Her immediate instinct is to curl up small, to clamp down on her emotions and tell Dan nothing. It was a long time ago, he doesn't need to know. But her gut knows that if she doesn't talk to him, it will always be there, a heavy shadow between them. Even if Dan doesn't sense it, she can feel it hanging over her. A constant 'what if' waiting to trip her up. And secrets have a knack of refusing to stay hidden; she's seen this time and time again.

"Yeah?" Dan is busy on his phone. "Work text. There, done."

"The other night, about abortions…"

"I'm sorry. I got the wrong end of the stick."

"The thing is…"

"What?" Dan's voice is sharp again. "I didn't misunderstand?"

"No, not that. I want this baby. Our baby!"

"So?"

"When I was 17. I…um…I got pregnant. It was early, I lost the baby." Julie can feel her words speeding up; if she doesn't get them out now, she'll never manage to tell him. "But we talked abortion. It wasn't right. He and I weren't right. I'd never have coped!"

Julie hears Dan suck in his breath. He's looking steadfastly at his hands, she can see his muscles tighten. Then he looks up.

"Christ, Julie, that's something. I…" Dan pauses, then starts again. "Thing is, my ex, she lied to me about being pregnant, then lied to me about aborting our baby. She wanted to hurt me. And it hurt a lot."

Julie reaches out her hand, tentatively resting it on Dan's shoulder as he gazes at the floor. "I'm sorry. That's shit, really shit."

"Lyndsay was cruel. She spouted all sorts about women's rights over their body, which I get. But not a word about my rights as a father. Then to find out she'd made it all up."

"And I tell you this! Do you hate me now?"

"No! I don't get it but…"

"You think it was wrong, bad."

"No. Yes. I mean I don't get it, I really don't get it. But it's not the same thing. And you didn't do it."

"No, but I think I would have, though it might have been the worst decision of my life."

"You wouldn't be you now if you had. It would have

changed you."

"And you wouldn't love me?"

"I didn't say that! Life's full of choices and changes."

"That doesn't mean it isn't true."

"Hell, Julie, I don't know. But that was you then, with someone else. I love you now, and our baby."

"Really?"

"Isn't that obvious?"

"I guess. It does haunt me, you know, what happened with Tom. Whether I would have gone through with it… That's why I tried so hard at university. Had to make it all mean something."

"Turning bad to good?"

"Maybe."

"My past haunts me too. Not just Lyndsay, my own stupid things."

"Yeah?"

"When I was seventeen, I spiked my sister's boyfriend's drink. I didn't realise he had work the next day and was driving home. Luckily, she clicked and stopped him. She dropped him back instead. Mum hit the roof when she found out Kim had taken her car without asking. Kim took the shit for me, but, every time I read about a drunk-driver in the papers…"

"Life's so messy, so complicated."

"But also so beautiful." Dan kisses Julie's forehead and draws her to him. "Turning bad to good's another thing we have in common."

"I like that idea," Julie smiles.

"There's quantum worlds out there with all the things we almost did, but didn't. I'm sorry I got worked up."

"It's okay, I get it now."

"We should get you to the doctors, book in the scans and stuff."

"Yeah, I guess."

"You guess?"

"So much shit lately. I don't even know how I'm going to tell Claire. What if it's too good to be true?"

"Five tests say it's true!" Dan strokes Julie's hand.

"And telling Claire?"

"When we've been to the doctor, then we think about your sister. Okay?"

"It's not that simple."

"No, it's not. But, for all you know, this could help her open up and talk."

"But what if something goes wrong?"

"Why should anything go wrong? You must be nearly ten weeks already. And you know they said what happened to Ju was very rare."

"What do you mean?"

"I mean don't worry. Cot death doesn't run in families. Would most likely not have happened again to Claire and Gary, if they'd stayed together and had another."

"I wish they had."

"If your sister had taken it better… Not that her breakdown isn't understandable."

"I know. Can't blame Gary for giving up."

"Exactly. And she hasn't made it easy for you either."

"I'll say!" Julie grimaces.

"But it's not your fault. Not her fault. Not anybody's fault." Dan pauses, kissing her forehead. "We're going to have a baby, Julie, our baby."

"Yeah, we are, aren't we?" Julie feels her body start to relax, unclenching into Dan's gentle rocking. The ease of his presence spreads through the last remnants of her tautness. They're going to have a baby. Their baby! Hers and Dan's!

Almost automatically, instinctively, Julie places one hand on her belly and the other in her pocket to touch the photo of her mum and dad's wedding. As if somehow through her touch, they're all linked, her mum and dad still part of this. As if some of her parents' magic might rub off for her and Dan. As if, with a sense of family behind her, she can find the strength to talk to Claire, a way to ease the future, even if she can't undo the past.

Three Green Bottles…

"You should go see her." Dan opens the fridge door as if to hide from his words, and from Julie's face when he says them.

"How can I? If it was hard enough before…" Julie stares at the untouched toast on her plate, her thoughts awkward-cornered and jabbing.

"But she's your sister," Dan closes the fridge door carefully, so that he can gauge Julie's reaction. "Besides, not seeing her is eating away at you. And you don't have to tell her everything."

Dan places the milk carton and Julie's decaf coffee beside her plate. He gently rubs her shoulders and kisses the back of her neck. A brief smile warms Julie's face as she slowly stirs in a little milk. She hugs the mug's heat in her hands.

"Even if I don't, she'll know. She'll see it in my face." Julie looks up at Dan. "You do understand, don't you? It could break her again."

"All that's happened to you both is unfair," Dan reaches across to squeeze Julie's hand. "But the longer you leave it… you know it's only going to get harder, don't you?"

"You're right, I know you're right, but not yet, I can't. Ju was like a daughter to me, but she was Claire's life. This might tip her even further over the edge."

"But not telling her means not seeing her. And not seeing her is…"

"Is what?" Julie's face hardens at his abrupt stop.

Dan hesitates, wary of the sharpness in her voice. He strokes Julie's clenched hand, then softens his voice as if to take the edge off the glass jab of his unfinished thought and the force of his next words. "Is like giving up, cutting off your last family."

Julie doesn't speak. Refusing to look up at Dan, she glares into her coffee: light brown and unfrothed. She grips the cup tightly and takes a sip. It's lukewarm and sickeningly milky compared to the hot, dark bitterness that her tongue has grown used.

Cutting off her family: easy for Dan to say with his family still alive, and normal! Normal without trying, while everything in her life has been forced, worked for, shaped into something that fitted her so well, until Claire and Ju.

Her bloody sister! Drama and pain followed Claire around like a black cloud pissing on everyone else below. Even as she thinks this, Julie hates herself for doing so. With losing Ju to cot death, it's no wonder that her sister's taken refuge in insanity, using madness to shut out the reality. But what about those left to pick up the pieces, those without that escape hatch. She and Dan had their own pains. They should be celebrating now, not agonising over Claire's reaction.

Julie cuts her toast into triangles and tries to eat one. The squelch of it's too much. She pushes the plate away. Many things taste strange now. Everything that was routine before has been placed in contrast, so that every change to the once everyday and unnoticed is like playing scales on a piano with half its notes missing. Presence reinforced through absence and absence reinforced through presence, Julie thinks. Her thoughts turn to her mum and dad, and what they would have said. She can hear Dad's calm but serious voice discussing Claire's illness, see her mum's concern in agitated hand gestures and flitting facial expressions.

But then, if Mum and Dad were here, they would probably agree with Dan. If Mum and Dad were here, there'd be no way of hiding things from Claire. If Mum and Dad were here, maybe there would be no need to hide things from Claire. And none of it is Claire's fault. If only Claire could see that, if only she could…could pull herself together. And there it is again, Julie's guilty thought: her secret wish that her sister wasn't so needy, so easily broken. Anger and sadness battle inside Julie as she struggles with this realisation.

"Here, take this with you." Dan offers her a cereal bar from the cupboard as if in apology. "And make sure you get lunch."

"Yes, sir!" Julie mock-salutes.

"See you later."

"Yeah." Julie tilts her face up for Dan's kiss. Then she looks at her watch. They're both running late now. She stands up and grabs her coat from the hook. No time for idling thoughts, least of all about her sister.

Four Green Bottles...

"I'll get us some green tea."

Julie sits down, while Dan heads into the kitchen to put the kettle on. She looks at the scan. She, or he, is definitely there. Their beautiful blob so baby-like already. Stroking her stomach, Julie marvels at the curve of their daughter or son's spine, the smudge of skull, a flutter shape that might be a hand.

Outside the window, the street's quiet. Sun's playing hopscotch with the leaves. The bright flowers in next door's garden remind Julie of the snapdragons that she and Claire used to play with. They'd make them chatter like noisy finger parrots, or fight like rainbow wolves. Julie wonders if Claire still remembers this. Or the time Claire cut the hair off Julie's favourite doll. Julie's not sure she can actually remember that. But the incident's so clearly entered into the repetitive anecdotes of family history that she can see the silver flash of scissors sparking in sunlight and Raggy's yellow wool hair on the floor like a toy bonfire waiting for a match to strike and burn it.

Volatile and over-sensitive was how Julie once overheard Mum describe Claire to another parent. But things with Claire hadn't always been fraught. They had fun too, Julie thinks. She pictures their odd nights clubbing at the Star. Too many cocktails, not enough dancing, high heels made to kill. She's embarrassed now by some of the lads she was into then. Men without names, with more muscle than substance. But she misses the music and her body's unstoppable motion with it. Also, the laughter with Claire and their early morning toast, dripping butter across worktops, licking it from fingers, wiping it from each other's chins…

No clubbing now, no hours of dancing, not with her tiredness. And no chance of Claire laughing, not judging from Julie's last visit. Is it three months ago? The days have slipped past as fast as rainwater spilling from gutter to drain.

But Julie knows that keeping busy is also avoidance. Claire has always been the one person that Julie doesn't know how to handle. What if she gets there and Claire refuses to see her? Is that better or worse than Julie seeing Claire and having to tell her about the baby, then feeling guilty for her own happiness?

While Dan's at the sink, Julie pulls out her diary from the kitchen drawer, the one with the letter and number for Claire's place. Beside it, a short note in Claire's scribbled handwriting.

It

The thing I cannot write about
is like falling into welled darkness
towards a stone splash that never rises.

It's the day's howling bones
bumping into sharp edges
racing at me from familiar soft corners.

It's the monotone of old movies
when the gorgeous girl is tied to the tracks,
only then the reel breaks

before the hero can save her;
when frogs croak in every room,
friends' mouths speak in black feathers

and the ceiling rains pins.
It's waking without frost or snow
to find life is a sudden cold landscape.

Claire seemed confused when she shoved it into Julie's hand on her last visit. It read as bleak as hell to Julie, made her shiver with the same blackness that kept her in bed for days after Ju's death. Was that darkness a family weakness or something that lurked inside everyone?

Although Julie didn't recognise the poem, she assumed it was something Claire had found and copied. But the nurse she spoke to said it was Claire's own, part of her therapy. It was a small but good sign, the nurse said, that Claire was writing about things, about what had happened. Also, that she was starting to write reality not delusion.

The black feathers make Julie think of their dad's 'Cello Woman'. They also remind her again of Emily Dickinson's feathers of hope. How does that poem end? "I've heard it in the chillest land - And on the strangest Sea…"

"Here you go." Dan hands Julie a jasmine tea. Feathers of steam curl upwards, winding their scent around her face and fingers. She blows across the cup, softly rippling the liquid's surface. When she and Claire were small, their dad would blow across the top of his collection of old glass milk bottles, filling them with different amounts of water so they could hear how the sound changed. Her cup's too wide to sing like that, but, if it could, Julie imagines a full and rounded note.

"Can you believe it?" Dan exclaims, picking up the scan. "Glad I got one too. The girls in the office will be all over 'bean' tomorrow!"

"I bet." Julie smiles with an edge of wistfulness. More than ever she wishes she had Claire to share this with.

"You could always ring your sister." Dan's suggestion is gentle but firm as if he's read Julie's thoughts from her face. "I know it's been a while, and this is hard. But, if you can't face visiting, maybe a phone call?"

"Hmm." Julie's response is non-committal but she can feel Dan watching her. She tries to visualise picking up the phone and asking for her sister. The more she thinks about it, the more she misses her sister's voice. And by telephone, it would be less pressured, no need to definitely tell Claire anything about the baby, a chance just to see what mood her sister's in, if she's getting better, if time has finally started healing.

Julie moves to the corner of the kitchen and picks up the phone. She cradles the handset in her hand and taps in her sister's number, then places the phone down again. Five times, she starts to type the numbers, and stops. What if she rings but changes her mind when she hears Claire? After this length of time, with no easy words handy and so much proverbial water under so many proverbial bridges?

Water! Julie remembers how much they used to love playing 'Poohsticks' when they were little. How long Claire took: carefully selecting the right stick, trying to guess the right angle for throwing, complaining if she thought Julie had let go of hers a fraction of a second earlier than the countdown. For Julie, the thrill was in the laughter, the way her fingers seemed to know without thinking which stick they wanted, maybe also how annoyed Claire could get if she, Julie, won.

It was fun too though, both begging to take a picnic, both cajoling Mum or Dad to join in, both chiding their dad when he deliberately cheated with the counting; how, once they reached that part of the park, they'd both dart ahead to the bridge and run sticks across the railings to create a metallic music while they waited for Mum and Dad.

Looking down at the pad beside the phone, Julie finds she has sketched a pattern of interlinked flowers and leaves, their stems branching here and there into spirals but still winding unbroken down the page. She and Claire aren't 'sisters, such devoted sisters' any more. Maybe they never were for any longer than a few hours of play, clubbing, gossip. Maybe there are too many other things now that can't be forgotten. But they still have a shared childhood, shared time, those first days and months with Ju. And Claire is her baby's auntie. Whether or not Claire wants to play that role, Julie won't know, her baby won't know if she doesn't tell her sister. And what if one day Julie's child asks her about Claire but she can't explain?

Julie knows she has to do this. And she has to do it now, so that she and Dan can start planning properly for their baby. She presses the green phone symbol.

SOURCES

The following books and articles were used to research background information for *Always Another Twist* and and the earlier novella *Kaleidoscope* (told from the viewpoint of Julie's sister, Claire):

Cot Death Prevention Fact Sheet.
Foster Carers' Handbook.
www.brightonandhovefosteringhandbook.org.uk/Be-Healthy/cot-death-prevention-fact-sheet.html
Brighton & Hove City Council.

Death crash driver may have had heart attack.
www.thisislancashire.co.uk/news/6116753.Death_crash_driver_may_have_had_heart_attack/
Lancashire Evening Telegraph.

Down Came the Rain. A Mother's Story of Postnatal Depression.
Shields, B.
Penguin Books Ltd.

'Heart attack' of author in crash.
http://news.bbc.co.uk/1/hi/england/1990066.stm
BBC News.

"Hope" is the thing with feathers.
Dickinson, Emily
www.poetryfoundation.org/poems/42889/hope-is-the-thing-with-feathers-314
Poetry Foundation.

Infanticide Psychological and Legal Perspectives on Mothers Who Kill.
Spinelli, M.G. (ed.)
American Psychiatric Publishing, Inc.

Separated at Birth.
www.guardian.co.uk/society/2007/feb/12/mentalhealth.health
The Guardian.

Sudden Infant Death Syndrome.
http://patient.info/doctor/sudden-infant-death-syndrome
Patient UK.

Treating Postnatal Depression A Psychological Approach for Health Care Practitioners.
Milgrom, J, et al.
John Wiley & Sons, Ltd.

Acknowledgements

My thanks to the following for their encouragement, careful reading, feedback and editing suggestions at various stages of this novella's development (and the writing of the preceding novella *Kaleidoscope*): Matthew Pegg at Mantle Lane Press, Jonathan Davidson at Writing West Midlands, Charley Barnes at Mad Hatter Reviews, Cynthia Rogerson at The Literary Consultancy.

A version of the poem 'It' was first published on the Royal Philharmonic Society website in November 2014 as part of the 'Notes into Letters' music-inspired project run with Manchester Writing School at Manchester Metropolitan University.

This publication was supported using public funding by the National Lottery through Arts Council England.

Mantle Lane Press would like to acknowledge support from Writing West Midlands.

Mantle Lane Press is a subsidiary of Mantle Arts Limited, which receives financial support from North West Leicestershire District Council.